WILD BOARS' COOK

For Oliver, Tobias and Felix, my favourite wild boars

– M. R.

For Simon and Diane

– S. B.

PUFFIN BOOKS

Published by the Penguin Group: London, New York, Australia, Canada, India, Ireland, New Zealand and South Africa

Penguin Books Ltd, Registered Offices: 80 Strand, London WC2R 0RL, England

puffinbooks.com

First published by Henry Holt and Company, LLC, 2008
Published in Puffin Books 2010
1 3 5 7 9 10 8 6 4 2
Text copyright © Meg Rosoff, 2008
Illustrations copyright © Sophie Blackall, 2008
Made and printed in China
ISBN: 978–0–141–32933–8

WILD BOARS COOK

MEG ROSOFF AND SOPHIE BLACKALL

PUFFIN

This is Boris.

This is Morris.

This is Horace.

This is Doris.

They are wild boars.

They are bossy

and selfish

and stinky

and HUNGRY.

Boris is so hungry he could eat

35 hot dogs

and a bushel of bonbons.

CRUNCH CRUNCH CRUNCH

Bad Boris.

CRUNCH
CRUNCH
CRUNCH

Morris is so hungry he could eat
a pineapple upside-down cake,
ten pickles and a boot.

MUNCH MUNCH MUNCH

Naughty Morris.

Horace is so hungry he could eat
a pizza as big as the moon.

YUM YUM YUM

Horrid Horace.

YUM
YUM
YUM

Doris is so hungry she is eating

a cookbook.

But wait!

Doris has found a delicious recipe.

A recipe for the biggest,

messiest, stickiest,

gooiest, chewiest,

most delicious pudding

in the whole wide world.

Watch out, everybody.

Wild boars are making

a Massive Pudding!

First they measure out
the ingredients.

"Ten cups of sugar!"
shouts Morris.

"Five hundred
chocolate-covered chocolates!"
roars Boris.

"A gross of doughnuts,"
squeals Horace.

"And lots and lots of broccoli!"
shrieks Doris.

Everybody stops and stares.
Broccoli?
In a Massive Pudding?

"Sorry," said Doris.

(Almost) all the ingredients went
into a massive pudding bowl.

"It's too dry," sobbed Boris.

"It's too small," wailed Morris.

"I'm hungry," howled Horace.

So Doris added one and a half puddles,

a bucket of squishy butter,

26 bananas

and a squid.

Then started to whisk briskly.

All the boars joined in.

WHISK WHISK WHISK!

STIR STIR STIR!

COOK COOK COOK!

And out came the most beautiful
Massive Pudding in the whole wide world.

Now, do you think
Boris and Morris and Horace and Doris
sat with their hands folded
and their napkins in their laps?
Did they pass the biggest piece
to the wild boar on their left?
Did they say thank you
and chew with their mouths closed?

Of course not!

They gulped and grabbed
and smashed and snatched
and pushed and prodded
and choked and chewed . . .
And they ate that Massive Pudding
in ten seconds flat.

"Delightful," moaned Boris.

"Delicious," groaned Morris.

"Divine," burped Horace.

"It was my idea," said Doris.

And they all lived happily ever after
for five whole minutes.

Until…

"I'm still hungry,"
cried Boris.

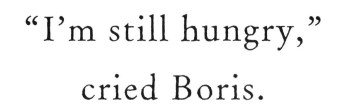

"I'm still starving,"
wept Morris.

"Everyone got more than me,"
howled Horace.

"Never mind," said Doris.

"I think I've found another recipe."

MASSIVE COOKIE
(makes one)

½ cup butter

1 cup sugar

1 egg

½ teaspoon vanilla

1 cup flour

½ teaspoon salt

½ teaspoon baking soda

½ cup chocolate chips

½ cup gumdrops

¼ cup M&Ms

Preheat oven to 375 degrees. Cream together butter and sugar. Add egg and vanilla. Stir in flour, salt, and baking soda. Add chocolate chips. Form into one large cookie on greased cookie sheet and decorate with gumdrops and M&Ms. Bake for about half an hour or until done. Do not attempt to make or devour the cookie without an adult present.